T0247004

THE BEGGAR STUDENT

ALSO BY OSAMU DAZAI

Early Light

The Flowers of Buffoonery

No Longer Human

Self-Portraits

The Setting Sun

THE BEGGAR STUDENT

BY OSAMU DAZAI

TRANSLATED BY SAM BETT

A NEW DIRECTIONS PAPERBOOK

Originally published in Japanese as *Kojiki gakusei*

First published as New Directions Paperbook 1618 in 2024
Manufactured in the United States of America

Library of Congress Cataloging-in-Publication Data
Names: Dazai, Osamu, 1909–1948, author. | Bett, Sam, 1986– translator.
Title: The beggar student / by Osamu Dazai ; translated by Sam Bett.
Other titles: Kojiki gakusei. English
Description: First New Directions edition. |
New York : New Directions Publishing Corporation, 2024.
Identifiers: LCCN 2024032067 | ISBN 9780811238588 (paperback) |
ISBN 9780811238595 (ebook)
Subjects: LCGFT: Novellas.
Classification: LCC PL825.A8 K5813 2024 | DDC [FIC]—dc23
LC record available at https://lccn.loc.gov/2024032067

10 9 8 7 6 5 4 3 2 1

New Directions Books are published for James Laughlin
by New Directions Publishing Corporation
80 Eighth Avenue, New York 10011

And in the realm of poverty,
Expect no wealth of decency.
                    – François Villon

THE BEGGAR STUDENT

Not even the wisest reader knows the anguish of the writer who has sent a truly awful piece of writing to a magazine in order to survive. Here goes nothing, I told myself, pushing that heavy envelope into the mailbox. It hit the bottom with a thunk. And that was that. Another crummy story. On the surface, it pretends to be a mirror to my soul, although I know as well as anyone the slimy worms of compromise are wriggling in the muck at the bottom.

It's a work in which the work is far from done. How about that infantile depiction of women? It makes me so ashamed I want to scream and run around in circles. I promise you, it's terrible. A lousy piece of trash. I have no right to call myself a writer. Such is my ignorance. No insights to impart. No illuminating views.

Among the literary set of nineteenth-century Paris,

the poseur writers were called "weather vanes" as a term of derision. Embarrassments to their so-called art, much like yours truly, they struggled at the salons to say anything of worth, hazarding comment only on the weather, hence the nickname. Yet stultifying as they were, these conversations took great effort; the weather vanes were just doing their best. And who am I to judge? The story I just dropped into the mailbox does no better.

Yesterday it snowed. When I saw it, I was stunned. A stunning sight. Opening the shutters, I found the world was sparkling a certain shade of silver – however, as I write this, wiping the sweat from my brow, I recognize how idiotic this must sound. Sparkle a certain shade? What's certain about that? All I do is stammer, incapable of making even one keen observation.

I am a shameful man. Honestly, I should've torn that lousy story into pieces and retreated to the mountains, never to return. But I'm so timid that I couldn't bring myself to do it. If I hadn't sent the manuscript today, I would've broken a promise to my editor. You see, I made the dumb mistake of promising to send the story to him by today at the latest. He even left space in the magazine for my atrocious story. And now I could be certain he was watching the clock tick, waiting for the packet to arrive. As crummy as it was, how could I tear it up and start again?

This makes me sound as if I've done the right thing and fulfilled my obligations. Sadly, no. I merely acted out of cowardice, afraid my editor would beat me up. If I'd broken my promise, I could've wound up with a busted nose. So, like a dead man walking, I cast aside whatever artistic fortitude I had, shut my eyes, and dropped that hideous manuscript into the mailbox.

And I call myself a man. Once the envelope went through the slot, it was all over. No amount of moaning could make things right. Soon enough, the story would be carried to my editor's desk. He'd drop everything to read it, only to wish he'd never seen the thing, but he would need to send it to the printer anyway, where skilled laborers with eyes like hawks and stolid faces would set type for my disastrous record of ineptitude.

It scared me to imagine what those eyes would find. Sloppy sentences full of errors. Ah, even the errand boy would double over laughing at my amateurish style. To think of all the precious paper that would be defiled because of me. My work will disgrace bookstore windows all across the land. Critics will sneer; readers will give up. That hack writer has outdone himself again, they'll say, setting a low bar for writers everywhere. Tough to beat.

One bogus line after another. Not one redeeming quality. I knew this all too well, and yet, resignedly, with trembling hands, I pushed that heavy envelope into the mailbox and heard it hit the bottom with a thunk. And that was that. But the misery that followed was beyond compare.

As soon as I had dropped that piece of garbage in the mailbox, the one by Mitaka Station, I found myself without the will to live. Head drooped, hands tucked into my sleeves, I kicked a stone down the path, lacking the discipline to go straight home.

Our house is in the middle of a stretch of farmland, about twenty minutes on foot from the station. Difficult to find; almost nobody ever visits. Most of the time, as long as there is no work to be done, I can be found wrapped in a blanket on the garden porch, too tired to read anything of substance, yawning my life away, maybe reaching for the newspaper to glance over the funny pages, where they run little quizzes, asking things like which of the following seven animals hatches from an egg: turtles, whales, rabbits, frogs, seals, ants, pelicans ... I might give this a moment's thought, but then I'll yawn so hard that tears will be running down my cheeks. That's when I'll gaze without a care at the sun setting in the fields beyond the yard, enjoying the existence of a man excused from living.

Considering my sorry state, I couldn't bring myself to make the walk back to our happy home. So instead, I headed in the opposite direction, toward the path along the banks of the Tamagawa Canal.

This was April, in the middle of the day. The canal was running deep and swift, while the cherry trees along the shore had given up their flowers, curling their green branches toward the water in a cool tunnel of leaves. A secret place, free of pretense. If only I could put that in a story. What a story it would be!

Here I paused, feeling a familiar urge to stop time and take in the scenery, but I was so ashamed of this onslaught of emotion that I allowed myself only a few brief glances down the bright tunnel of green as I clopped along the edge of the canal.

I started walking faster. Pulled downstream by the river. The dark water was dressed up with the rotting petals of the cherry trees. It rushed forth without a sound. Before I knew it, I was chasing the brown petals down the river. Trotting like a jackass. While the troop of petals might grow sluggish, or speed up, it never stopped, riding the stream with wily ease. At that point, I had passed Mansuke Bridge, at the entrance to Inokashira Park, but I continued following the water, utterly transfixed.

This was the part of the canal where once upon a time, a kind teacher by the name of Matsumoto Kundo drowned while trying to save one of his students. The river had always been narrow, but back then it was deep and had a mighty current. That's why people in the area gave it the fearsome name Maneater Brook.

I was starting to get tired, so I gave up chasing petals and looked into the water. The troop drifted away, slipping off into the full glare of the sun, then out of sight. I let out a nihilistic sigh and wiped my palm across my brow, which is when I heard a voice down in the water.

"Whew, that's cold!"

You can imagine my surprise. This nearly knocked me off my feet. A pale-skinned naked boy was swimming in Maneater Brook. No, not swimming; he was being pulled downstream.

Lifting his face from the water, the boy grinned at me from ear to ear, as the current dragged him away.

"Whew, that's cold! So cold."

This is a disaster! He's going to drown! So what if I can't swim, I can't just let him die! I'm going to die someday, may as well be now. There's no choice but to try and rescue him. Even if it means the both of us will drown. I guess this is the end . . .

Such were the absurdities that buzzed around my brain as I ran like crazy down the riverbank. In a word, I'd gone hog wild. Barreling forward – not even wincing when I tripped over a tree root and nearly fell onto my face.

Normally, I avoid grassy areas at all costs, because they're full of snakes, but in this case I made an exception, since why should I fear venom when I'm about to drown? I was on a mission, saving this boy's life, but as

I tore through the tall grass of the riverbank, I heard a howl erupt behind me.

"Yow! My stomach. You practically stepped through me."

The voice sounded familiar.

Stomping to a halt, I turned and saw the swimmer sprawled out naked in the grass.

I lost my temper.

"Watch out! This river isn't safe," I yelled, realizing my rebuke was rather late, then I smoothed the sleeves of my kimono, trying to regain my composure. "I've come to save you."

The boy sat up, squinting his steely eyes so that his long eyelashes almost met.

"You're crazy, you know that? Didn't even look before you ran me over. Blowing steam out of your ears. Well, look at this. Your geta left two fat lines on my stomach. See? That's where you stepped on me. Like a big equals sign. Look at me!"

"I can't. You're indecent. Go on, compose yourself. It's not right for a boy your age to laze about with no clothes on. Have some manners."

The boy put on his trousers and stood up.

"Are you some kind of a park ranger?" he asked.

I pretended not to hear this. What an idiotic question.

Then the boy smiled, baring his white teeth.

"Can't imagine what you're so upset about," the boy

said evenly, then stuffed his hands into his pockets and walked over to where I stood. A single cherry blossom petal clung to the wet skin of his right shoulder.

"This river isn't safe," I told him. "You can't swim here."

I was repeating myself, only this time in a deeper voice, almost a growl.

"It's dangerous," I said. "That's why it's called Man-eater Brook. On top of that, it feeds into the Tokyo waterworks. They're gonna have to sanitize the whole thing now, because of you."

"I know, okay?" the boy said, tightening his cheeks into a guilty smile.

Up close, his features were more striking than I'd originally thought. Tall, elegant nose, turned up slightly at the tip. Thin eyebrows. A pair of big, round eyes. Small mouth and modest chin. Even with that pale complexion, he was the picture of a handsome youth. Of average height and build. His hair cropped short, no peach fuzz on his face ... while his narrow brow was marked by three stacked wrinkles, and his nostrils were embellished by deep grooves where his nose met his lips.

The result was that he resembled a monkey. Perhaps no longer a boy at all, but a young man. In any case, he sat down in the grass and looked me in the eye.

"Care to join me? Hey, when you get mad like that,

you look kinda like a samurai. From another time. Maybe the Ashikaga period, or the Momoyama period. Centuries ago. Do you remember which came first?"

"I'm afraid I don't."

I crossed my arms behind my back and paced around, losing my composure.

"Well then, can you name the tenth shogun of the Tokugawa shogunate?"

"I'm afraid I can't!"

And I genuinely could not.

"You don't know anything. Guess you must be a teacher?"

"I'm afraid that you're mistaken. I'm –" I started, but I hesitated for a moment, then quit being such a wimp and spat it out. "I write stories. I suppose that I'm a writer."

After the words had left my mouth, I wished I'd never said them.

"Writer ..." said the boy, thoroughly unimpressed. "In that case, writers must be pretty dumb. Hey, you ever heard of Évariste Galois?"

"I think I've heard that name somewhere before."

"Bah. I'll bet all foreign names sound the same to you. You only think you've heard it before, but you haven't. Proves how little you know. For your information, though, Galois was a mathematician, not that you'd appreciate his work. Now, that was one smart man. Shot dead at twenty. You might try reading a book sometime, since you don't know doodly-squat. Okay then, so do you know about the tragic death of Niels Henrik Abel?"

"Is he another mathematician?"

"Lucky guess. Abel was even smarter than Galois. He died at twenty-six."

A wave of anguish nearly knocked me off my feet. This was too much. I left the boy behind and found my own place in the grass to lay down and be alone.

When I closed my eyes, I heard hibari tweetle in the sky:

> *Though cheeky as a younger man,*
> *He never gets them laughing anymore.*
> *Like a wrinkly old monkey*
> *Nothing about him to adore.*
> *If he keeps deathly quiet*
> *They take him for a fool,*
> *And if he opens up his mouth*
> *They tell him to save his breath.*
>
> – François Villon

I opened my eyes and shouted to the boy.

"My problem is that I lack conviction!"

"Who asked you about conviction?" the boy yelled from his own bed in the grass, cutting me down. "You'd have to be at least as smart as Galois to make a claim like that."

This kid found fault with everything I said.

There was a time when I was just like him. A time when a new fact or skill would burn a hole into my brain, and I'd need to show it off, or else the world would end. My guess was that the boy had spent the night before, perhaps even that morning, skimming through a book about great mathematicians who died young. If he told me that Galois had swum up a vicious current in the nude, it wouldn't have surprised me in the least.

"Did this Galois by any chance go swimming in the nude one April morning in some book you read?" I asked him, trying to get the upper hand.

"What are you talking about? You dummy. You're hopeless, you know that? This is why I hate adults. All I was trying to do was teach you something new. Trying to do you a favor. But you're convinced that being older means you're always going to be right."

I was incensed. This time, the boy had made himself an enemy.

ろ

It was decided. I would thrash the boy for all his insolent remarks. This required me to step into the role of a vicious, nasty man. I'll have you know, I may look like an ass, but I'm not a total moron, and when I say I lack conviction, I only mean it relative to my own high standards. I would take the boy to task. What else was I supposed to do? Sit back and let a kid without even a loose grasp on reality treat me like a simpleton?

I stood and slapped the dust off my kimono, then turned my nose up at him.

"Listen, boy. Don't try to fool me with your psychological techniques. That's such a cliché. Somebody with real intelligence would know better than to put on airs like that. The only idiot here is you. Okay, Mr. Big Talk? You must've been bullied pretty bad. No one in their right mind would admit to even knowing you. Just a lonely, little boy with nowhere to go."

The boy was reclined in the grass with his eyes closed, laughing away, but then he squinted at me, looking skeptical.

"What are you saying? None of this applies to me, you dimwit."

"Well then. Beg your pardon."

I bowed my head at him, before I realized what I'd done. Shit! Bowing to one's foe in the midst of a debate was a beginner's error. On the battlefield, all manners are verboten.

It would seem my gracious nature had become a handicap. Same goes for my attempt to come across as a cool customer, when I was anything but. In times like these, I tended to prioritize swagger over actual results. A surefire way to lose a fight. Nothing to be proud of. But I pulled myself together.

"Would you mind standing up?" I asked. "I've got something to say to you."

In my mind, a scheme was taking shape.

"You sound upset," he said. "Guess I don't have a choice. I hope you're not trying to bully me."

I found his every word repellent.

"I might say the same to you," I told him. "Who's to say which one of us has the upper hand? Come on, get up and put your coat on."

"Gosh, you really are upset," he said, grunting and groaning as he stood. "I've got no coat to wear, though."

"I know you're lying. Pretending to be poor. That's the cheapest brand of heroism there is. Go on then, put your shoes on. Come with me."

"I don't have shoes," he said. "I sold them."

The boy looked up at me and smiled.

I was besieged by a queer horror. Overcome with the suspicion that the boy in front of me was, yes, a complete and utter lunatic.

"Don't tell me you're –" I started saying, but I couldn't get the words out. It was too rude a thing to ask. Already on the verge of tears, I was afraid how he might answer.

"I had a pair till yesterday. Didn't need them, so I pawned them off. Still got a shirt, though."

His tone was innocent. Reaching into the tall grass, he grabbed a camel-colored undershirt of admirable quality.

"You think I walked all the way here in the buff?" he asked. "My room's over in Hongo. Man, you sure are dumb."

"You walked here barefoot?" I asked, overcome with doubt and increasingly uncomfortable.

"That's a tough trip over land." He pulled the shirt over his head. "Lord Byron said the only time his bum leg didn't bother him was when he was swimming. That's why he loved being in the water. And really, honestly, when you're in the water, who needs shoes? Much less a coat. The lines between high class and low, between rich and poor, magically dissolve," he said, deploying the words with rhetorical flair.

"Are you Lord Byron?" I asked, doing my best to kill his spirit. His bloated speech was getting harder to endure. "Unless I've missed something, you don't have a bum leg. Besides, a person can't spend their entire life doing the breaststroke."

My comeback was so hostile and predictable that it sent shivers down my spine. No choice but to fight fire with fire, I told myself, trying to justify my inelegant behavior.

"You're jealous." The boy touched his tongue to his lower lip. "Clearly you envy me. When a feeble idiot encounters youthful genius, it drives him crazy. He needs to shut down every single thing the young guy says to feel superior. But there's no use trying to reason with hysterics. If you've got something to say to me, I'm all ears. Man, you're a real coot. Hope you're not trying to drag me off somewhere."

Next thing I knew, the boy had stepped into a pair of geta. They were basically brand new, much finer sandals than the pair that I had on.

Noting his genteel choice of footwear, I felt strangely

relieved. Like I'd been spared. I know it's shallow, but I can't help feeling wary of a person if their choice of dress is too eccentric. For ages, first-rate poets have worn shabby clothing as a point of pride, and personally, I have no interest in fashion, wearing whatever clothes my family lays out for me. I try not to concern myself with the way other people dress, but this can only go so far, and if I'm honest, the idea of someone wearing nothing but an undershirt and pants, without a coat or shoes, is positively horrifying to me. Blame it on my shallow and uncultured sensibility. Once I'd seen this boy dressed in that sumptuous shirt, however, and wearing wooden sandals much more stylish than my own, I felt extremely relieved. His clothes may have been nice, but they were absolutely normal.

Lunatic? Hardly. In that sense, I was fully justified in proceeding with my scheme. He was an ordinary boy. No harm in a bit of sporting debate, even if we did cross swords.

"I'd like for us to have a proper conversation," I said, working my cheeks into an artful grin. "You act like I'm uneducated, like I'm some kind of an imbecile, but at least I'm doing something with my life. And even if I am an uneducated imbecile, I'm still much better off than you. You're in no position to look down on me. After all this unjust abuse, I have no choice but to retaliate."

Quite an impressive takedown, if you asked me.

Too bad it only set him off.

"Man, you sure are desperate for a playmate. Hmmm ... I tell you what, how about you buy me lunch? I'm starving."

Hah!

I was this close to laughing in his face, but somehow, I bent the smile into a frown.

"Don't hide it," I warned the boy. "There's no way some part of you isn't terrified. Let's get moving."

Discombobulated and afraid that I might burst out laughing, I kept ahead of him and made sure not to turn around.

My scheme was too simple to even call a scheme.

At best, it was a vague intention.

There is a little teahouse run by an older couple, set in the perfect spot on the shore of Inokashira Pond. Whenever a friend visits our house in Mitaka, which isn't often, I almost always take them there. You see, for whatever reason, I have considerable trouble entertaining guests at home. I'm too anxious to communicate. These visitors are so intelligent and erudite that a transcript of their idle conversation could be published as a treatise on existence, whereas I, the rusty weather vane, can manage nothing but a series of inelegant grunts, fidgeting in my seat, at most lobbing a stock response like "Wow," which does more harm than good. And so, lest I endure the scorn of family members who might overhear me through the paper doors and look up from their sewing in disgust, I usually cut my losses and propose to take my guests out for a little stroll. And when inevitably that fails to loosen up my nerves, I'll bring them to the teahouse on the shore of Inokashira Pond.

Once I'm cross-legged on one of the long, wide benches at the teahouse, I feel my brain begin to hum. Alive. Comfortably perched and sipping a cup of oshiruko, or maybe amazake, looking out over the pond, I marvel as my speech relaxes, finding myself, yes, at last, in full command of every thought, and able to expound on a variety of subjects that I know nothing about, the master of a heightened state of mind that knows no bounds.

It would seem that this phenomenon has something to do with the fact that, as a rule, my friends and I set our eyes on the pond as we converse. Stated plainly, we're all looking at the same thing, without so much as glancing at the person we're talking to.

You ought to try this out sometime, dear reader. Sit yourself down on the sofa of a coffee shop or bar, facing the fireplace beside the madam of the house, so that the both of you are staring at the flames, and talk as if you're speaking to the fire – I promise, up against even the dullest mind, you'll be able to sustain a lively conversation for hour after hour. But take heed, reader:

you must not look into each other's eyes, not even once.

At those benches in the teahouse by the pond, it's by doggedly fixating on the surface of the water that I'm able to unleash my eloquence. As long as I can battle my opponents in the venue of my choice, I can hold my own against a wit as sharp as Diderot or Sainte-Beuve without suffering too much of a disgrace, although my lack of learning would, I suspect, set me up for defeat. Especially because I can't speak French as well as any of those guys.

And so, it was my plan to bring the boy down to the teahouse for a lethal dose of my vituperative banter. He had made a mockery of me. I had no choice but to set him straight.

Keeping ahead of this self-styled youthful genius, I led us down the wooded paths of the park, brimming with conviction. Ready to show him what a feeble idiot could do.

It would appear that our walk through the park had made the boy uneasy.

He was talking to himself.

"My mother's dead, you know. And I'm too embarrassed to tell you what my father does for work. It's unforgivable. I'm just a country boy. No time to worry about manners. Wish I could get my hands on a pistol. I'd take potshots at the power lines and blow them all down, one by one, *bam, bam*. Japan's so small. When

I feel sad, nothing cheers me up like swimming naked. Hey, what's the problem? You couldn't stop me if you tried. All this blather. Skip the sermon. Nobody called a priest. I've read this story before. Come on, leave me alone. My name's Goichiro Saeki. I'm not good with numbers. I prefer a decent ghost story, if I'm being honest. Ghosts only show up thirteen different ways, you know. Or wait, if you count when a paper lantern says hello, there's fourteen. Who cares, though. Anyway ..."

The boy went on and on, spewing this nonsense.

Pretending not to hear him, I led us through the trees and down the stone steps, across the grounds of Benzaiten Temple, and down the path in front of the zoo, then walked for a few minutes more, skirting the shoreline of the pond, until we reached the entrance to the teahouse.

I was feeling mischievous. Snickering with glee. The boy had told me I was looking for a playmate. He was right: in the pit of my stomach, I could feel the squirming worms, up to no good. But on top of that, I felt a writerly desire to understand the younger generation, which prompted me to close the space between us.

Big mistake.

And thanks to this mistake, I was soon forced into a string of hapless, chilling, and disgraceful hardships.

Arriving at the teahouse, I took my post cross-legged

on a bench and cast my gaze out over the pond, chuckling to myself. I was in good shape. Or so I thought.

The boy sat cross-legged beside me, knees wide apart. After I ordered us two cups of oshiruko from the old lady in the kitchen, he turned to me and asked casually, "Think they have oyakodon, too?"

I panicked. All I had in my kimono sleeve was a single fifty-sen note. Handed to me on my way out the door by a family member who insisted that I get a haircut. But once I'd dropped that worthless manuscript into the mailbox, the imaginary critics in my head bellowed and laughed with such authority that I withered at the thought of visiting the barber.

"Hold on, hold on," I hollered to the kitchen, feeling hot all over. "How much for the oyakodon?"

"That would be fifty sen," the lady said.

"All right, let's make that one oyakodon. Just one. Oh, and a cup of tea."

"Bahaha!" The boy laughed in my ear. "Now that's what I call thrifty."

I sighed. It was pointless trying to respond. The gloom consumed me. How could I one-up him if my pride was bruised so badly? I didn't even want to speak.

"Are you a student?" I asked him in a friendly tone, making the smallest small talk possible. Meanwhile, my eyes were trained, as usual, on the bright surface of the pond. A red carp paddled over the rocks, barely two feet from the wood legs of the bench.

"I was a student. Until yesterday," the boy said, sounding relieved. "Today I'm free. School's just a waste of time."

"Maybe so. Though I'm not so fond of weighing in on people's personal affairs. In my experience, it never does the other person any good."

"Some hero you are. All you do is make excuses. What a load of crap."

"Crap, huh. Well, that's too bad. There were so many things I'd hoped we could discuss, but I've lost interest. Perhaps our time would best be spent in silence, taking in the view."

"Easier said than done. I couldn't shut up if I tried. The only way I can stand being alive is if I'm playing the buffoon."

The boy spoke in a mature voice suffused with sincerity.

"What's that from?" I asked, looking right at him.

The boy scowled.

"From? From me. Who else? Up until yesterday, I was a tutor for a respectable family. Teaching algebra to their pea-brained daughter. Not like I know enough to teach. I just picked it up as we went along. Which worked okay for a while. But if you start asking me to sing for my supper –"

He didn't finish the thought.

は

The old woman brought the boy's lunch on a platter.

"Go on," I said. "Eat up."

The boy blushed.

"Aren't you going to have some too?" he asked, sounding like a different person.

His big eyes looked into mine.

"I'm fine," I told him with the utmost disregard, sipping on my tea as I gazed out on the trees across the pond.

"It looks delicious," he said in a quiet, humble voice.

"Enjoy," I replied dryly, not wanting to embarrass him, then returned to my tea, watching the trees across the pond, as if I had no interest in him whatsoever.

The zoo was somewhere back behind the trees.

A savage shriek carried across the water.

"That's a peacock you just heard," I said, "the peacock's cry."

I turned slightly toward the boy, who had set the
bowl of chicken, eggs, and rice between his legs. Head
down, he mashed both eyes with the back of his right
hand, holding the chopsticks.

He was crying. What was I supposed to do?

Pretending not to notice, I turned back toward the
water and pulled a pack of cigarettes out of my sleeve
to have a smoke and calm my nerves.

"My name . . ." the boy said in a ragged voice, really
sobbing now. "My name is Goichiro Saeki. Remember
that. Someday, I'm going to repay you for your kind-
ness, you'll see. You're a good person. Look at me, all
teary-eyed. This happens sometimes when I'm eat-
ing. The bad thoughts hit me all at once, bringing me
down. I'm embarrassed to tell you what my father does
for work. He . . . teaches elementary school, out in the
country. Been at it over twenty years and still hasn't
been promoted to principal. Doesn't have the smarts.
It makes it hard for him to face me, his own son. His kids
make fun of him. Calling him 'Mr. Sack.' I can't let myself fail the way he did. I need to make it in the world."

"What's so embarrassing about teaching elementary school?" Realizing that I'd raised my voice, I
pursed my lips. "If things don't work out for me as a
novelist, I'll probably wind up teaching at a rural ele-

mentary school myself. Those are the only two jobs I could stomach doing, or could undertake with any real enthusiasm."

"Don't you know anything?" Now the boy had raised his own voice. "In a small town, the teachers need to keep the rich kids happy. Just like the principals and village leaders. It's a racket. Don't even get me started. That's why I don't like teachers. I wish I could just study whatever I want."

"So study then. What's stopping you?" Petty as it was, I hadn't yet forgiven him for making fun of me. "Where's all that piss and vinegar now? Huh? The only coot around here is you. Men aren't supposed to cry. Come on, boy, blow your nose and pull yourself together."

Eyes on the surface of the pond, I reached into my sleeve for a pack of tissues, which I tossed into his lap.

The boy laughed and gave his nose a mighty blow.

"I'm not sure how to put this," he said. "It's weird. If I study hard, trying to please my dad, I get so incredibly stressed out. This voice inside my head keeps asking: is this really the right time to be debating abstract mathematical concepts? To be asking whether a quintic equation can be solved algebraically, or if you can define the sum of a divergent series? As one of my best tutoring students said the other day, the nail that's sticking out gets hammered down ... It's usually the stupid kids who say this kind of thing, the ones who never study. But coming from him, it put me in the weirdest mood. Maybe he's right, maybe this isn't the right time for esoteric journeys of the mind. We're living in an age of jousting, not debate. I find it so depressing."

"Sounds like a lazy reason to drop out of school. Not to mention spineless. I bet you're the kind of guy who wishes a big earthquake would just turn the whole world upside down."

Feeling energized, I launched into another zesty sermon.

"You're confusing a bad day with a bad life," I assured him. "No faith in the natural tendency toward universal order. I'm paraphrasing Valéry, of course."

I closed my eyes, pretending to be gathering my thoughts, then opened them and struck a rather pompous tone.

"Since time began, those with even a minute ability to think for themselves have regarded laws, systems, and customs with antagonism and contempt. Which makes sense, because ridicule and satire can be immensely satisfying. But one must be aware of just how slippery and dangerous satire can be. It dispenses with responsibility. As tedious as laws, systems, and customs might appear, freedom and reason would dissolve without them. It's like standing on a big old boat and complaining about what a hunk of junk it is, though if you happened to go overboard, you'd be a dead man, period. After all, freedom and reason don't just pop up out of nowhere. By which I mean, there's no freedom in nature, and nature is no friend to reason. That's what makes reason so effective. It can throttle nature, conquer nature, giving human beings their agency. One might call reason the glue that holds society together. In that sense, the order we enjoy is artificial, but we need this artifice if we want to go on living. Look, I can see why the grim state of the world would make you want to abandon your studies, but really, can't the grim state of the world serve as a motivator, as a reason to affirm your trust in order, on a universal scale, and to complete your education? Researching the sums of a divergent series, or an elliptic function, or what have you, takes a certain kind of hero, to be sure."

After this coup de grâce, I glanced over at the boy, who was innocently chewing on his food. Judging by his expression, he had barely listened to my speech.

"Well, what do you say?" I asked him, eager for approval.

The boy looked up and swallowed.

"Is this Valéry guy French?"

"That's right. He's a first-rate cultural philosopher."

"If he's French, then I'm not interested."

"Why not?"

"Because they're losing the war."

The boy's big eyes betrayed no sign of tears. Dark pupils cool with laughter.

"French is the language of a ruined nation," he explained. "Your problem is that you're too nice, know that? I mean, whatever kind of order this guy Valéry is talking about, it isn't universal anymore. He's clinging to an antiquated notion. Way too proud of being French. That's why they're going to lose."

"Come on," I said, shifting in my seat. "That's hardly fair."

"Order, of the right kind, though, is a beautiful thing."

Ignoring my objections, Saeki spoke with gravitas and a twinkle in his eye, holding the donburi in one hand.

"I can't trust the order of a Frenchman," the boy said. "But I can trust the order of a mighty army. What I want is an order verging on brutality. Like having someone tie you to a post. That's why everyone I know can't wait to go to war. Who wants a lukewarm independence? Not much different from a leash. I'm telling you, we're under lock and key. Too much more of this and I'm gonna lose my mind. Being stuck here, on the home front, messes with your head. It's tough."

"Listen to you! You'll stop at nothing to avoid a hard day's work. A moment of patience is worth a thousand boasts."

"More like a single deed is worth a thousand words."

"And where's that gotten you? The only deed you've done is swim up Maneater Brook buck naked. Know your place."

That's it. I'd won.

"It's not like I do this every day," the boy said.

Then he laughed, sounding tired and much older than he was.

"Thank you for lunch," he said.

Bowing politely from his seat, he set the empty bowl off to the side.

"Something's bugging me. Mind if we talk it over?"

"Go ahead."

I was in it deep now, up to my ears.

"Not like I'm expecting it to help at all," he said, "but here goes. Lately, I've been all mixed up. My parents could only pay my way through middle school. Because we're poor, okay? I was on my own. But I wanted to keep studying mathematics. So I took the high school entrance tests, without telling my dad, and sure enough, I passed. Do you know Keizo Hayama? He was an undersecretary of the railways a while back. Practices law."

"Never heard of him."

My irritation was so potent that it nearly left me blind. I guess I have no patience for listening to people talk about themselves. I try to listen, but in no time, every thought is overshadowed by the question of what any of this has to do with me. I feel the burden of responsibility, as the unease and discomfort tax my sanity. Even if I feel bad for a person, I'm certain of the cold hard fact that I can't do anything for them, which leaves me feeling even worse.

"I don't know any lawyers," I confessed. "Is he rich?"

"You could say that." The boy was awfully sedate. "We're from the same town. It's a funny thing to have in common. All it means is that our accents are the same. Anyway, Hayama used to give me a little bit of pocket money. But not for free. For giving lessons."

"A tutor and a tutee both, I see."

I was ready to be done with this. Not even slightly interested.

"No, I mean, he's got a daughter," Saeki explained. "In her third year at a school for girls. Shaped like a dumpling. Useless kid."

"Ah yes. Do I detect a hint of romance?"

Now I'd really gone off the deep end.

"Don't be ridiculous," the boy scoffed. "I've got my pride. Lately, this Hayama guy's been treating me like I'm his lackey. And his wife's just as bad as him. But then yesterday, I hit a breaking point –"

"Sorry, kid, but that's life. No such thing as a free lunch."

I regretted having spent so much time with the boy.

"Gee, you must've had it off real good as a kid," he said. "Guess you never had to bite your tongue and earn a buck." The boy was proving tough to beat. "I bet you can't even wrap your head around the concept of hard work. Life's not so easy for the rest of us."

"I'm well aware of all that," I told him, "thank you very much. The difference is that I know how to keep my mouth shut."

"Okay then, big fancy writer, think you could narrate a movie?"

"Narrate?"

"Yeah, so over spring break, this guy's daughter visited Hokkaido and came back with reel upon reel of 16 mm film she'd wasted on the landscape. It's an epic with no story. She's only shown me part of it, but it's obviously just one bland slice of realism after the other. They're gonna do a screening of it in the parlor at Hayama's house. Inviting all his daughter's so-called friends. But here's the thing. They've asked me to be the benshi. I mean, narrate it then and there, in front of everyone. To keep things interesting."

"Sounds fun." I laughed out loud. "You kidding me? Spring in Hokkaido, a bit of snow glazing the hillside –"

"Are you crazy?"

The boy's voice hummed with anger.

I stiffened my cheeks into a dour expression.

"Hardly," I said. "I could do that in my sleep. It takes an egomaniac like me to play the fool convincingly. I can't believe you'd pawn your uniform over a thing like this. Talk about hysterics. No wonder you were splashing in the river. Anything to avoid facing the facts."

"Easy for you to say. But there's no way that I can do it. And you, I think you're full of it."

He almost got me there.

"Well, what's next for you then, kid? You figured that out too? Can't go splashing around in cold rivers forever. Sounds like maybe it's time to head back home. Get yourself on your feet again. But a word to the wise: don't get stuck on these childish ideas of right and wrong. And this benshi job? It's going to be fine. Just one night of stage fright, then it's over. One fell swoop. Hell, maybe I should do it for you."

These last words were my undoing. Now I'd really stepped in it. Being told that I was full of it must've really hit a nerve, because the next thing I knew, I'd volunteered for something that I couldn't weasel my way out of.

"Think you could handle it?" he asked me.

"Handle it? Of course I can!"

Well then.

An hour later, this kid and I were walking down Jingu-dori in Shibuya. Like a couple of fools. Mind you, I was thirty-two years old. Old enough to know better. But there I was, running this ridiculous errand, because I didn't want a boy to think that I was full of it. In that sense, I was a victim of my own childish compulsions.

The whole thing made me terribly uneasy, but rational-
izing the setup as an act of mentorship made me feel
better. Like I was teaching him a lesson. Leading him
back onto the path.

When I first heard the boy drowning in the river, I
made up my mind in a flash: even if I couldn't swim, I
had to try to save him. It was my civic duty, or at least
that's what I was currently trying to convince myself.
As it turned out, saving him didn't mean water rescue,
it meant dressing up in a schoolboy's uniform and hat
and attending a soiree at the Hayama's in his place.

Hey guys, I'd say, I'm Saeki's friend, he isn't feeling
well, I'm filling in for him, then I'd take the stage and,
to the best of my ability, narrate that waste of celluloid
otherwise known as *Early Spring in Hokkaido*, keeping things fun and interesting for all those friendly
faces.

It's not like I had a schoolboy's uniform on hand.
And neither did Saeki. Or, he used to have one, until
yesterday, but he evidently sold it off, even his shoes.
We'd have to find another schoolboy who'd oblige.

Saeki seemed doubtful of my dedication, even re-
luctant to continue with the plan, but his hesitancy
sparked in me a manic burst of energy that gave me the
momentum I needed to proceed.

I'd practically dragged him by the arm out of that
teahouse by Inokashira Pond, stopping at my family's

house in Mitaka for just long enough to shave the stubble from my face (instantly younger) and to grab a bit of cash, which I dropped into the sleeve of my kimono.

I asked the boy if he had any friends who had a uniform to spare. He said he knew a guy in Shibuya who might, so we went down to Kichijoji Station and took the Teito Electric into town.

Was I losing my mind?

That's how we made it onto Jingu-dori. Clickety-clacking in our geta.

Turns out the screening at Hayama's was that very night! No time to lose.

"We're here," the boy said, stopping at a sleepy building.

Looked like a boarding house.

White magnolias dangled like fists from an old wooden fence.

Cupping his hands, Saeki yelled up to a row of paper windows on the second floor.

"Hey, Kumamoto!"

"Let's go, Kumamoto!" I cried, joining in the fun.

Not a care in the world.

Like I was back in school.

Trust me, Wagner,
There is no policy
Like honesty.
If you are moved to speak,
Speak your mind readily.

       – Goethe's *Faust*

"Coming!"

The gentle voice that answered from behind the paper windows had a girlish earnestness that left me feeling strangely disappointed. I'd hardly expected any friend of Saeki's to be soft-spoken. Kumamoto was a name with heft. A boy with such a gentle voice ought to have a softer name, like Aomoto.

Our friend Saeki, meanwhile, shouted in the gruff sort of voice one might expect from a guy named Kumamoto.

"It's Saeki! Okay to come up?"

"Sure," the friend said.

Boy, he sounded gentle.

I couldn't help but laugh. Saeki guessed what I was thinking.

"This guy's a dilettante," he whispered, giving me a wink. "Typical bourgeoisie."

Not missing a beat, we raced each other through the front door of the boarding house and pounded up the stairs.

Saeki tried sliding open the paper door to his friend's room, but a tremulous voice stopped him.

"Wait a second!"

The voice was just as high-pitched as it sounded from the street, only now it had a sternness to it, like the boy was braced for combat.

"Just you, or both of you?"

"Both of us," I answered carelessly.

"Saeki, who's that you brought here with you?"

"Not sure."

Saeki gave me a bewildered look.

It occurred to me I hadn't introduced myself.

"Takeo Kimura," I whispered. "Takeo Kimura."

It's true. Dazai is just a pen name. I was born Takeo Kimura. Growing up, I found the name incredibly embarrassing, so despite being a string bean, I've been publishing as Osamu Dazai, a name that makes me sound like a street fighter who might break your neck.

Which is great ... though, as you can see, if I'm really put on the spot, I often wind up blurting out the old name that my parents gave me.

"The name is Takeo Kimura, if you please," I said, feeling sufficiently embarrassed.

"Takeo Kimura," Saeki echoed, nodding. "Yeah, just me and Takeo Kimura."

"Takeo Kimura? His name is Takeo Kimura?"

Kumamoto sounded skeptical. I was in agony. At that moment, Takeo Kimura felt like the stupidest name in the entire world.

"That's me, Takeo Kimura," I said, tripping over my own tongue. "We've come to ask if you could do the two of us a favor."

"Please don't," said Kumamoto. An unlikely reply. "Meeting new people makes me awfully nervous."

"So sue me for bugging you," Saeki grumbled, but his friend beyond the paper door heard him just fine.

"Bug is right. That's precisely the problem. A bug bit me on the nose. It wouldn't do to make a new acquaintance with my face like this. First impressions mustn't be taken lightly."

Hilarious. This kid had us in stitches.

"You idiot," Saeki said.

The former student threw open the door and barged inside. I staggered after him, holding my belly in a failed attempt to stop myself from laughing.

In a corner of the room, the only light coming in

through the paper windows, a boy with perfect posture and a buzz cut sat on his heels, dressed in a dark blue kimono splashed with flecks of white.

One look at his face, and I knew he was an Aomoto, without a doubt. None of the brawny swagger that the name Kumamoto brings to mind. Pale round face, bleary eyes blinking behind round glasses, like a moleish Harold Lloyd. The nose in question did, in fact, appear to be a little red, though nothing so grotesque as he'd suggested. Quite the chubby fellow, a roly-poly boy. A little shorter than Saeki.

Self-conscious about his appearance, Kumamoto hastened to fix the lapels of his kimono.

"Saeki, aren't you being a bit pushy?" he asked, completely serious. "Not even my own parents have seen me in this awful state."

The nose.

He turned away dramatically.

Saeki sidled up to Kumamoto, wiping the smile off his face.

"Doing some reading?" he inquired.

There was a big book (horizontal text, not characters) open on the low desk, but Saeki swept his hand across the floor and picked up a little paperback.

"*Tale of Eight Dogs*, huh. Interesting choice, Kumamoto . . ."

Standing over him, Saeki riffled through the little

book. "You're always leaving books you don't read open on the desk and hiding what you're really reading underneath. You sure have funny habits."

Saeki wasn't smiling. He tossed the paperback onto Kumamoto's lap.

This made Kumamoto so upset that I couldn't help feeling sorry for the guy. He blushed and covered the small book with his hands.

"Quit hassling me," Kumamoto said through gritted teeth, almost too quietly to hear.

He shot Saeki a deathly glare out of the corner of his eye.

I was sitting cross-legged in a corner, laughing to myself as the two of them went at it, but Kumamoto looked miserable. I had to intervene.

"*Tale of Eight Dogs*, huh? That's a classic. You sure have ..." *A nose*, I almost said, but remembered this was a sore subject. "*An eye*, you've got an eye for quality literature. Some call that the first Japanese novel."

"It's true," said Kumamoto, pursing his red lips. "I've been reading it again, in bits and pieces."

"Hahaha!"

Saeki stretched out on the floor next to the desk and cackled like a gremlin.

"How come you always say you're reading stuff *again*? Be honest, you're still at the beginning."

"Quit hassling me!" Kumamoto said once more,

considerably louder than the first time. His choice of words was simple and refined, though I could see the tears in his eyes.

"Saeki, don't tease," I said. "Of course a scholar and a gentleman like him has read *Tale of Eight Dogs* before."

As much fun as it was to watch these two boys spar, I was painfully aware that we had business to attend to.

"Well then, Kumamoto . . ."

Doing my best to shift the mood, I proceeded to ask if I might borrow his school uniform and hat for the evening, well aware that it was an impertinent request.

"My uniform and hat? Why mine?"

Kumamoto scowled and turned to Saeki.

"I wish you wouldn't hassle me like this. Who's this guy, anyway?"

"Never mind, forget it!" Saeki yelled at him from the floor. "No one's forcing you to help us. And for the record, it's *you* hassling *us*. Okay, Kumamoto? This guy's a good person. Not egotistical like you."

"Hold on," I said, bristling at being labeled a good person. "I'm plenty egotistical. Saeki wasn't too fond of the idea of borrowing a uniform, but I insisted that we come here. I'm happy to explain, just understand that I'm the one who's asking for the favor. It's only for one night. I'll return it first thing in the morning."

"Suit yourself," said Kumamoto. "Honestly, I couldn't care less."

Really sobbing now, he turned his back on me and

started rifling through the big book open on the desk.

Saeki sat up.

"Forget it," he said. "Let's get out of here."

"Don't be silly!" I shook my head. "At this stage of the game, backing out would make you no more than a coward. Was coming here some kind of joke or what?"

No sooner had I started quarreling with Saeki than Kumamoto turned toward us and crossed his arms, grinning like this was, in fact, a joke.

"Would you mind telling me what's going on here, Saeki?" Kumamoto asked him in a tone of grandiose superiority. "What sort of mess are you in this time?"

"Forget it. I never should've asked you." Saeki sprung to his feet. "I'm going home."

"Hold on." I stood and grabbed his arm. "You aren't going anywhere. Kumamoto never said we couldn't borrow his uniform. I'd call you a spoiled brat if I thought that you were listening."

Watching me tear into Saeki put Kumamoto in an even better mood.

He stood up, looking smug.

"Exactly right. You spoiled brat. I never said you couldn't borrow it. And by the way, I'm not the least bit egotistical."

From a hanger on the wall, Kumamoto took down a uniform and hat and handed them to me with expert care, like he was lending me one million yen in cash.

"Here you are."

"Too kind." I caught myself midbow. "Now, if you'll excuse me, I'll get changed."

So I got changed.

Excuse me! There was no excuse. This was an abomination.

My arms were at least six inches too long for the sleeves.

The pants fit like a pair of knickerbockers. Way too baggy, not to mention short. They barely covered up my knees, leaving my hairy shins for all to see.

I couldn't help but laugh. A broken, raspy hum.

"Give me a break," Saeki said, laughing in my face. "Not exactly a good fit."

"He's right," said Kumamoto. Crossing his arms behind his back, he looked me up and down, giving me a full appraisal. "I'm not sure what sort of clothes you make a habit of wearing, but I hope that you won't mention getting those from me."

He sighed, flaunting his distress.

"It's good enough for me," I said. Wishful thinking on my part. "I've seen students dressed like this in Hongo, by the university. They say eccentric clothing is a sign of genius."

"The hat won't even stay on his head!" Saeki jibed, ready to comment on my every fault. "At this rate, he may as well narrate the movie with no clothes on."

"That hat is not the least bit small, thank you very

much." Kumamoto was quite particular about his things. "And my head's an average size. The same, in fact, as Socrates."

Sideswiped by this preposterous boast, Saeki and I both burst out laughing. Pretty soon, Kumamoto caught on too, and the whole lot of us was cracking up. There was an all-too-welcome change of atmosphere. We three had reached an understanding. It made me want to take our little party to the streets of Shibuya. There was loads of time before the sun went down.

Borrowing a furoshiki from Kumamoto, I bundled up the kimono I'd been wearing and handed it to Saeki to carry.

"Let's get moving. Come on, Kumamoto, join us for a cup of tea?"

"Kumamoto's busy studying." Saeki made it clear he wasn't happy that I'd asked the other boy to come along. "He has to finish reading *Tale of Eight Dogs* . . . again, that is, in bits and pieces."

"Far from it. I'm not busy." Kumamoto seemed eager to join us. "Things are about to get interesting. You're like Dr. Faust after his youth has been restored."

"Faust, huh? I suppose that would make Saeki here Mephistopheles." I was having so much fun that I forgot how old I was. "In his heart of hearts, the poodle is a wandering scholar. Get it? Ha!"

I gave Saeki a knowing look, but the eyes that I

found looking back at me were bloodshot. Swollen, red with tears. I wondered if something about our plans was bothering him. Without another word, I gave him a soft pat on the shoulder and stepped out of the room.

If I wasn't sure before, I was sure now: I would be this boy's salvation.

Out of the boarding house, we took our sweet time heading toward Shibuya Station. The people on the streets of Tokyo didn't seem suspicious of my costume. Kumamoto, in his blue kimono, wore a pair of felt-soled zori and was carrying a cane for show. Rather effete of him, if you ask me. Saeki, dressed the same as earlier, carried my old clothes in the bundle, while I was doing my best to look normal in the tiny uniform and geta, like a growing schoolboy with no money for new clothes.

We were soaking up the sun of that gorgeous April afternoon, prowling the streets.

"Let's stop for tea," I said to Kumamoto.

"Fine by me. We're almost there. As long as we steer clear of any girls. What with my nose so red and all. First impressions mustn't be taken lightly. If I meet a girl today, she's likely to assume my nose has been this red for my entire life and will continue to be red for the remainder of my days."

Listen to him. Dead serious.

I thought this was absurd, of course, although I kept my laughter to myself.

"Right, then, how about a milk bar?"

"Who cares where we go?" Saeki said. Despondent for some time now. Like a poodle that had lost its will to live. Flopping one foot down after the other, heavy on his feet. Falling behind and catching up. "Asking somebody to stop for tea is a great way to get rid of them. That's how it's gone every time somebody's blown me off. First, you have a cup of tea."

"What on earth are you saying?" Kumamoto spun around to face Saeki. "Quit talking like a crazy person. We're having tea because we're building a connection. Pure and simple. *Tale of Eight Dogs* brought us together."

The boys were one step short of fighting in the street. I'd had enough.

"Cut it out, guys. Both of you. You're friends, remember? Saeki, cheer the hell up. At least Kumamoto has manners. He's trying. Unlike some people. It's not nice to laugh at someone when they're clearly doing their best."

"You're the one who keeps laughing at him," Saeki said, turning on me. "A sly old fox, that's what you are."

Once he and I were arguing, it could go on forever. Luckily, there was an unassuming restaurant just ahead.

"Let's go in here and have a decent conversation."

I took Kumamoto by the arm and headed for the entrance. The poor kid was white as chalk and trembling all over. Saeki caught up, though not exactly hustling.

"Stay back, you fiend!" Kumamoto cried. "They only let him out of the cell yesterday, didn't you hear?"

This got my attention.

"No, I'm afraid Saeki failed to mention that."

Too late now. We were passing through the curtains at the door.

ほ

I was speechless. Realizing that I'd been betrayed, that I'd been taken for a fool, was like swallowing a bitter pill that went straight to my head and knocked me off my feet. I deposited myself at a table in the corner of the restaurant. Kumamoto sat across from me. And that punk Saeki, lagging behind, came through the doorway long enough to throw the bundle at my head and run away.

That was the last straw. I chased the urchin out into the street, where I caught him by the left arm, dragging him inside. Driven by a savage need to take him down for making such a fool of me, I felt my weakness transform into strength.

Saeki wriggled, trying to escape.

"Have a seat," I said, leading him by the shoulders to a stool.

Saeki flailed his limbs and tore himself away from me. Once he was out of reach, he pulled a glinting object from his pocket.

"Want some of this?" he asked me in a gravelly voice that sounded wholly unfamiliar. As you might imagine, I was stunned – convinced, for a moment, that I was going to die.

When something pushes me over the brink of fear, I have a nasty tendency to begin laughing like an idiot. A disturbing, wild laugh. I lose control, can't hold it in. An expression not of brazenness, but extreme cowardice that takes me to the limits of delirium.

"Hahahaha!" I laughed. "Think you're gonna scare me with that swashbuckling pose, when mere seconds ago you were squirming like a worm? I've seen this play before. The villain has to wave his knife around or we'll forget he's there."

Saeki took a step toward me, adjusting his grip on the blade, but Kumamoto put him in a bear hug.

"That's my knife! Let go!" he cried in a voice shrill enough to sting the ears. Not exactly the line I was expecting. "Saeki, you're terrible. You took this from my desk drawer, didn't you? Not even asking for permission. It's my policy to give people the benefit of the doubt, so I'm not going to say you stole it. This is your chance to give it back. I love that knife. The idea was to lend your friend my hat and uniform, not give you free rein over all my private possessions. Give it back! That was a present from my sister. I love that thing. Give it. Hey, stop waving it around. That's not just any knife. It's got a little pair of scissors, a can opener, and three other tiny tools. It's delicate. I'm begging you, please give it back."

Kumamoto wailed; his speech as strained as ever.

That rapscallion Saeki must have been touched by his friend's desperate plea, because he let his arms fall to his sides, devoid of energy, as a wry smile crept over his pallid face.

"You can have it. Here, it's yours," he said, like this was all a joke. Avoiding eye contact, Saeki handed the Swiss Army knife to Kumamoto, then plopped down on a stool. "Whatever you say, bucko."

Now he really sounded like a scoundrel. His rough language spoiled the mood and put me, once again, in a sad place.

I took the seat beside him.

"Goichiro," I said, using his first name for the first time, then filled the silence with a sigh. "There's no need to get upset. This side of you surprises me."

"Stop cooing in my ear. I'm gonna barf. Must feel great sermonizing to a loser like me."

Saeki spat out the words. Grimacing, he flopped his arms onto the tabletop, so sullen he could barely close his fingers into fists.

I almost lost my patience.

"You're a real pain in the neck," I told him, speaking my mind.

"So what if I am?" he said, quick as ever to talk back. "Like I just said, skip the sermon. Go away, leave me alone."

The boy was staring at the wall, eyes glazed over with tears. Seeing him this way, I once again found myself unable to speak. Kumamoto was across the table from us, giving his beloved knife a scrupulous inspection. Once he was satisfied that the delicate treasure had been returned unmolested, he wrapped it in a handkerchief and dropped it in the right sleeve of his kimono, then looked up at the two of us with refreshed curiosity.

"Well, what's all this about? I have a sense of what you're saying, Takeo Kimura, and of what Saeki has said as well, although I'll have to ask you to elaborate," he told us, sober as a judge. "Well then, shall we have ourselves some coffee? Or a bite to eat? Let's put an order in. Once we've had a chance to talk things over, I think we can arrive at some kind of an understanding."

Kumamoto was ready to sit back and let us come to blows, offering a serene nod now and then, maybe a stock reply, but Saeki, seeing through his games, was not going to let this slide.

"Not a bad time for you to head back home, Kumamoto." Saeki's voice was calm, but he was nowhere close to smiling. "You've got your knife. Kimura promised to return your stuff first thing. Hey, don't forget your cane."

Kumamoto, though, was almost gushing tears.

"No need to hassle me like that. I only have your best interests in mind."

I found his earnestness endearing.

"Exactly," I said. "After all, Kumamoto, I wouldn't be wearing this uniform and hat if it weren't for your most generous assistance. Frankly, you've been indispensable. I think it's best for you to stick around. Three coffees, for the boys."

I yelled our coffee order back into the kitchen, where a boy of thirteen, maybe fourteen, had been staring at us for some time now.

"Mom's gone off to the baths," the kitchen boy answered in a trailing drawl. Too young to be in high school like the others. "She'll be back soon."

"Ah, I see."

Caught off guard, I turned to Kumamoto.

"What shall we do?" I whispered.

"Let's wait," he said, unperturbed. "There aren't any girls here, so I'm nice and comfortable."

Apparently, his red nose was still bugging him.

"Why don't we have a beer instead?" asked Saeki, popping out of the woodwork. "Look at all the bottles they've stashed back there."

I peered out back, and sure enough, the wall was lined with big bottles of beer. It was a tempting prospect. I could use a beer. That just might neutralize the caustic tension in the air.

"Hey," I hollered to the kitchen boy. "Let's have some beer instead. I'm sure that you can handle that without your mother's help. All we need's three glasses and a bottle opener."

The boy nodded reluctantly.

"I won't be drinking," Kumamoto said, returning to his snooty tone. "Alcohol's a vice. I prefer the joys of scholarship, taken straight."

"None of us," Saeki snapped, "is forcing you to have a drink. Spare us the silly excuses. We know the only reason you don't drink is that your sister doesn't let you."

"What, now you're some kind of boozehound?" This time, Kumamoto wasn't backing down. "Knock it off. I'm warning you. Rumor has it you were drinking beers the night you got arrested. Word's out, Saeki, all over school. Everybody knows you got locked up."

The kitchen boy brought us a tall bottle of beer. When he placed a cup in front of each of us, however, Kumamoto turned his upside down.

This nearly pushed me over the edge.

"He's right," I said. "None for you either, Saeki. I'll drink the whole bottle myself. Alcohol's a vice, no truer words. You'd better steer clear while you can."

Midsermon, I popped the cap and poured myself a glass, kicking it back in a single gulp.

It was delicious.

"Ah, tastes awful," I lied, hoping to smooth things over. "Truth be told, I don't like alcohol, but beer's okay. You barely get a buzz." There I was again, making excuses for myself. "Last thing I'd want to give up are the, you know, joys of scholarship," this last part added in a cheap attempt to butter Kumamoto up.

"Too true," said Kumamoto, spirits buoyed. "We're like a couple of Parnassians."

"Parnassians," Saeki mumbled. "Ivory tower."

His words were almost too quiet to hear. Coming from his mouth, they had an oddly painful ring; barbed hooks driven straight into the heart.

I drank another glass of beer.

"Goichiro," I said in a voice rich with compassion. "I understand what's going on. When you walked in and chucked the bundle at my head and ran away, everything clicked. So you left out a few key details? Fine. That's fine. I don't blame you. Blame tends to work both ways, after all. I understood, but couldn't say so right away. So I played dumb. Now that I've had some beer, however, the alcohol working its magic, I'm able to speak up. Or, if you think about it, we actually have you to thank. Since you're the one who pointed out the beers."

"Of course," said Kumamoto in a low voice. "When

Saeki mentioned the beer, he was thinking far ahead. Of course . . ."

"What kind of idiot would do something like that?" Saeki laughed. A nervous laugh. "I was just . . ."

Faltering, he rubbed the table with both hands.

"I understand, okay?" I assured Saeki. "You were just trying to show me a good time. No, that's not it, not quite. More like brightening the mood all around. You've known your share of hardships, Saeki, and it's made you sensitive. You notice things. You're considerate. Unlike our pal Kumamoto over here, who only thinks about himself."

Riding the buzz, I gave Kumamoto a gentle jab.

"That isn't true," he said, baffled by my sneak attack. "It only looks that way to you."

Kumamoto hung his head and muttered a few words, although I couldn't understand them.

I was starting to enjoy myself. One might say I'd cleared my mind.

This prompted me to order us another beer.

"Goichiro," I said, turning myself, once again, toward Saeki. "No hard feelings. After all, who am I to blame you?"

"I wish you would." Now there's the Saeki I thought I knew. "Always offering excuses for why everything is fine. Well guess what, Takeo Kimura, we're sick of it. You're a grown man. Act like one. Quit hemming and hawing. If you're mad, then yell at us, no holding back.

Adults are always sugarcoating things to cheer kids up, as if the whole world really did come down to love and understanding. It makes me sick."

Saeki swung his head away from me.

"That's not, I mean, okay . . . you've got a point."

I smiled. Like a maniac. He got me! My heart ached so bad you'd think that it was being clawed apart, but the old fox that I was, I hid my feelings.

"Saeki, as much as I can sympathize with the real pain behind your accusation, I can't accept the basis of your argument. Truth is that grownups are the same as kids, except a little worse for wear. Kids ask a lot from grownups, but grownups ask at least as much from kids. It's a real mess. But it's the truth. We count on you to hold it all together."

"I don't believe this," Kumamoto said. Incredulous, he cocked his head as if I were a pitiable sight. Me!

"People are tricky. We're a mess." I inhaled another glass of beer. "To put it gently, we're always one step away from being completely overwhelmed. To put it harshly, we're all babies who can't take a word of criticism. I know that I've been floating big ideas like love and understanding, but I'm just trying to help you guys build confidence. Okay? And what do I get in return from you but scorn! If only I was sure that you could take it, then I'd give you a good talking-to and tell it like it is, but from the look of things –"

"It's pointless," Saeki said. He was done listening.

"Enough is enough. Keep your proverbs to yourself. If you want to teach us something, exercise some self-control."

"He's right," said Kumamoto, looking relieved. "Besides, who trusts a drunk to tell the truth?"

He squeezed his cheeks into a condescending smile.

"Okay. I messed up," I admitted, feeling a cool pain reach my stomach. "But I'm not hopeless. Drinking's not a regular thing for me. And I'll have you know, I give myself a rubdown with cold water every day."

Aware of how bizarre this must have sounded, I felt the heat of panic burning right behind my eyes.

"Enjoy youth while you can!"
Goes the advice of a great sage,
And I, a fool, believed the man.
(Don't force me to relive the pain)
But wait! On the next page,
He adds with a straight face:
"Childhood is but a lie;
the golden years, frivolity."
                              – François Villon

Long ago in Paris, a woeful excuse for a man named François Villon had a hissy fit that he recorded for the ages in his testament.

"Alas! If only I devoted those mad years of my youth to an education, striving to become a member of society, by now I'd have a home to call my own, a warm place to sleep. What a fool I've been. Storming out of the schoolhouse like a spoiled brat. The memory of these choices is enough to tear my heart asunder!"

At this point in my life, I'll admit that Villon's lamentation strikes a chord. I'm unable to fend off even the mildest affront, like when Kumamoto smiled condescendingly and told me that he couldn't trust a drunk.

What the hell was I thinking, telling these boys of my daily rubdowns with cold water? Running my mouth yet again. And the worst part is that I was just doing my best.

I lack the finesse of the politician, the nerve to shout out orders, the education necessary to teach others in a way so that they'll actually learn. I've been trying to take good care of myself, but the most that I can show for it is daily rubdowns with cold water. Yet, I assure you, for a knave like me, this is a major undertaking.

I must say, these two boys and all their condescending smiles made me painfully aware of my incompetence.

It would appear that Saeki had found the sight of me holding the glass of beer, lost in thought, too pitiful to bear, because he offered me these words of consolation.

"No need to fall on your sword," he said, looking into my eyes. "I'm sorry, okay? You get what happened. I was embarrassed. Wouldn't let myself tell you the truth. I'm no liar. There's just one thing I lied to you about. The screening. It was actually two nights ago. The narration went off without a hitch. And afterward,

I sold my uniform and shoes, then went out for a couple of beers, when I was spotted by the cops –"

"Say no more."

Looking up at Saeki, I waved my hand as if to brush off his confession.

"You're not to blame. Did what you had to do. My fault for insisting we go through with it. I should have got the hint when you were hesitant to make the trek to Shibuya."

I sighed. A heavy sigh. Getting it off my chest.

"Yeah," Saeki said, nodding sheepishly. "There was no time to set things straight. It all comes down to me not wanting to admit I was associated with that sappy film. That's why . . ."

Once again, Saeki nervously rubbed the tabletop.

"That's why I lied," the boy said. "I'm sorry. I figured that you'd hate me if I told you that I'd been locked up. You'd realize I'm no good. This Hayama guy, he's done a lot for me. No part of me wanted to narrate that idiotic picture show, but I figured that I owed it to him, as a sort of parting gift, so I got up there in front of all those schoolgirls and gave them a performance. Then after it was finished, I was mortified. Felt like my life was over. Like there was no hope for a man like me. Pour me a glass of beer, huh? It feels good to open up. Almost too good. You're a great man, Takeo Kimura, you know that? A guy who's not afraid to show the weakness of his heart is a guy that you can trust – that's what I say. The fact that you'd spend time with us, not sitting on some high horse, but coming down to our level, listening, commiserating . . . it means a lot. I know I can't let things go on like this. I'm gonna study, I'll make something of myself, you'll see."

Saeki stood and poured all three of us a frothy glass of beer. Determined in his bearing.

"Kanpai," the student said. "You too, Kumamoto. Let's have a toast to the good times, no shame in that. As long as you're not drinking to wash away the pain!"

"I suppose one glass won't hurt," said Kumamoto. No match for Saeki's acute enthusiasm, he stood reluctantly. "I'm not sure why we're doing this, but I guess I'll join you for a glass."

"Why do this?" Saeki asked in disbelief. "What more reason do you need! I'm turning things around. Aren't you happy for me? Man, so egotistical."

"No, that's not it," Kumamoto said.

This time, the young man stood his ground.

"I like to have a thorough understanding of what's happening. Cause and effect. You won't catch me at a banquet for a cause I don't support. Reason is my guide. I'm a man of science, after all."

"Listen to him!" Saeki scoffed. "Man of science? Anyone who says that doesn't know the first thing about science. You're just using science as a false god. Proof of how little you know."

"Boys! Boys!"

Now I stood up.

"Kumamoto's just embarrassed. You've made him sore with these relentless theatrics. Like any intellectual, he's sensitive."

"He's a clown," Saeki said under his breath.

"Let's have that toast," said Kumamoto, who seemed to be at his wit's end. "Beer makes me sneeze. That's what I meant by cause and effect."

"Sure it is."

Saeki laughed.

I laughed too.

Kumamoto wasn't laughing. Glass of beer in hand, he raised it to eye level and used his free hand to adjust the neck of his kimono.

"A toast to Saeki, for turning things around. Hope to see you back at school tomorrow."

His voice was plaintive, almost maudlin.

"Thanks, Kumamoto." Saeki nodded once, politely. "May you always be this kind and gallant."

"Saeki, Kumamoto, each of you has your flaws. But hey, I'm flawed myself. Let's find a way to help each other out."

Feeling openhearted and alive, I raised my frothy beer over the table.

Our glasses clinked; we drank them down.

A second later, Kumamoto let out a real honker of a sneeze.

"Okay," I said, "one toast for good times is enough. Can't be using good times as an excuse for getting soused."

As much as I was ready for another glass of beer, I felt oddly compelled to pause and make a mental record of the way the room felt in that moment, the impulse strong enough to mute my thirst.

"Well then, from now on, you two better stay away from beer! As the great Carl Hilty tells us, a true student of culture won't fall victim to the worst evils of drink. Which means you're fine. In fact, a little sip now and then is beneficial to your health. But since the other kids at school and common laborer types can't help themselves, they drink so much they run the risk of pickling their livers. So I implore you – for their sake! – don't set a bad example. Not just for them, no, no. Do it for us. We came of age in dark times, to be sure. Given a bad education, force-fed a diet of the worst ideas. Times in which a love of drink has been a badge of pride, of righteousness. 'Let's drink to that!' etc. It's all but futile trying to outrun these woeful habits. All you can do is try though, right? If you boys set a good example and build clean, positive habits, the rest of us, disgusting vermin that we are, will follow suit. So yield not to temptation. Onward and upward. Well then, that's enough generalization for one day. I can't seem to make it through a simple thought. Not even things the sloppiest of books get right. You see, it's no good leaning on broad adjectives like *clean* or *strong* or *positive*. I wish I could just cut my belly open and let all of the words come spilling out. No matter if it's gibberish, as long as it's my flesh and blood doing the talking. But I digress. These big ideas leave a bad aftertaste. I'll get off my soapbox now."

Kumamoto clapped. A nice round of applause.

Saeki was grinning ear to ear.

I switched back to my usual tone of voice.

"Saeki, I've got about twenty yen in change on me. Use it to buy back your uniform and shoes. That'll take care of appearances. Then swallow your pride and head over to Hayama's house. Make things right. Next time life gets you down, curl up in a blanket in your rented room and open a good book. What finer way to spend your youth. A bit of hardtack for the belly, and it's time to get to work. We got a deal?"

"Anything you say." Saeki was blushing big time, but his tone was strong. "Just so you know, though, when you talk like that, you look just like a samurai. Like you're from another century. Meiji days."

"Yeah, well, maybe he has samurai blood in his family tree," said Kumamoto, just like him to make such an outrageous observation.

It took effort not to laugh.

"Kumamoto, use this twenty yen to buy back Saeki's things."

"Who needs that junk?" Saeki growled.

Blushing hard. At this point, he was crimson.

"Hold on, nobody's saying that you'll get them back today. Your friend Kumamoto will hold them for you until you're ready to resume your studies."

"Gladly." Kumamoto took the money, beady eyes shining like marbles through his round spectacles.

He stood up tall and started with a speech of his own.

"You can count on me, Takeo Kimura. Until a new day dawns on Saeki's –"

"Thanks, Kumamoto, that'll do."

My patience had evaporated. I was to blame for bringing money into this.

"Let's get going," I said. "We can take a little stroll."

And so we did.

Outside, the streets were dark.

Evidently, I was the only one intoxicated.

Forgetting I was dressed like a poor schoolboy, I'd been blabbing on and on about one foolish thing after the next.

"Hey, Saeki, isn't that bundle heavy? Let's take turns. Toss it over. Got it! Great. *Al-ter-na-ti-ve-ment.* That's how the French pass something heavy back and forth. Flaubert spent three hard months deciding on that as the last word for a story."

This had turned into quite the evening. Who knew that life was full of such surprises? Staggering through the streets of Shibuya that night with these two students, I'd managed to step back into a youth I thought I'd lost. My exhilaration knew no bounds.

"Let's sing a song. How about it? Us three, all together. Ready? *Eins, zwei, drei.*"

> *Where have you gone, my youthful days*
> *Now but a memory for me to hold*
> *Each night I chase forgotten dreams*
> > *All the way home*
> > *All the way home*
>
> *My cap is stained, my pants are torn*
> *My gleaming sword's rusty and rough*
> *The forks are bent, the bottles roll*
> > *All the way home*
> > *All the way home*
>
> *A boyish heart never grows cold*
> *It knows the way through work and play*
> *And when the band empties the stage*
> > *We'll have the song*
> > *We'll have the song*
> > > – Alt Heidelberg

Nobody sang but me. I belted out the lyrics, screaming each line like I had nothing to fear. At the end of the song, I called them out for not singing along.

"Hey, you guys didn't even sing! Let's try that again. *Eins, zwei, drei.*"

"Hey. Hey."

Someone tapped me on the shoulder of my uniform.

When I turned around, I saw it was a cop.

"It's after dark. Can't have you boys causing a stir. Where do you boys go to school? Well, then? Answer me. Come on, now, spit it out."

I could feel the hands of fate upon me. I'd been caught. In his heart of hearts, the student is a thirty-two-year-old drunken poet. This was going to take more than an apology to fix. It was all or nothing. Time to run.

"Hey. Hey."

Someone was yelling at me.

I came to.

Sprawled out on the grass.

The sun high in the sky.

Hibari flapped and tweetled overhead.

Things started to come together. I was lying, like before, on the banks of the Tamagawa Canal in Inokashira Park.

Turning toward the voice, I saw that it was Saeki.

Crouched beside me in the grass, wearing a college uniform.

Shoes, dress shoes, polished to a glassy sheen.

"Hey, I'm heading out," he told me unexcitedly. "How can you fall asleep like that? You bum."

"Asleep? Me?"

"Yeah, you conked out halfway through the story of poor Niels Henrik Abel. Like some hermit of the fields."

"Really?" I smiled sadly. "I was up all night last night, finishing the story. Not a wink of sleep. It must've just caught up with me. Was I out for that long?"

"Maybe ten or fifteen minutes? Brrr, it's getting cold. I'm heading out. See you."

"Hold on." I sat up in the grass. "I thought you went to high school."

"Of course I did. How else would I have gotten into college? Boy, you're dumb."

"When did you start college?"

"This past March."

"I see. Your name is Goichiro Saeki, right?"

"Who's that? Sleep's made you even stupider," he said.

"I see. Tell me then, what made you want to jump into this river naked?"

"It looked like a good time. What more reason would I need?"

"Okay ... This might sound weird, but you've got a friend named Kumamoto, right? Proud little fellow."

"Kumamoto? Hmmm ... Nope. Is he in engineering too?"

"Different guy. Was it a dream? I was hoping we would meet again ..."

"What are you saying? Sleep's gone to your head. Shape up. I'm going home."

"So long. Hey, one more thing –" I said, detaining him a moment longer. "Study hard."

"Thanks for the tip."

He stood briskly and departed. Leaving me scarcely able to contain my desolation. In the back of my mind, I could hear myself belting out the last line of the final refrain.

We'll have the song.

A forgotten dream.

I got up and started walking toward the teahouse. Rummaging through my kimono sleeve, I found that I still had the fifty sen.

My thoughts returned to the toast we'd shared. A toast to the good times.

Saeki, Kumamoto, each of you has your flaws. But hey, I'm flawed myself. Let's find a way to help each other out.

I would've loved to head straight down to Shibuya and go back to the place we drank those beers, but I only knew the way from Kumamoto's boarding house. The memory was hazy. Must've been a dream after all.

Emerging from the wooded section of the park, I passed the zoo and walked around the pond to the old teahouse. When I sat down inside, the old lady came out to greet me.

"Just you today? That's a first."

"One bottle of Calpis, please."

I wanted to drink what the kids were drinking. I wanted to feel young.

Sitting cross-legged on the bench, I took little sips of Calpis, but I knew I wasn't a kid anymore, just a lousy writer, thirty-two years old. And the milky soft drink didn't make me feel the least bit young.

We'll have the song, always.

All I could do was sit there with a rueful smile on my face, pondering that line.

Eins, zwei, drei.